9 781387 561537

A special thank you to the Hunterdon County Cultural and Heritage Commission.

Thank you to The Amistad Commission of New Jersey, the Elizabeth Historical Society, and Dr. Spencer Crew.

I am especially grateful to my support circle: John G. Tucker, Joyce Claiborne, Chessie Dentley Roberts, Lynn Roberts, Gayle Brandeis, Pablo Cartaya, Peter Catalanotto, Brooke Vitale, Malik Whitaker, Wanda Croudy, Arlene Campbell, Joy Ogunyemi, Jane Rockman, Leonard Bethel, Veronica Bethel, Leon Coleman, Vicki Coleman, Rhonda Stewart, Nicoline Evans, Melinda McPhail, Jacki Belin, Barbara Seater, Lori Moog, Sharon Decker, Rijni Chopra, Lou Palmer and The Martin Luther King Youth Center of Bridgewater, Nancy Field, Monique Christian, Myra Thomas, Richard Peters, Anita Rosenblithe, Gordon Bond, Noelle Williams, and Yolanda Seiley-Ruiz.

Lisa Michelle Tucker, a Professor of English, teaches at Raritan Valley Community College.
Malik Whitaker is a teaching artist, graphic designer, and a fine arts painter.

This book is dedicated to the Chessie Dentley Roberts Academy #30 in Elizabeth, New Jersey.

"It's an *acute* angle!"

Mrs. Humphrey smiled. "Right again, Chessie. Now, who can classify this triangle?"

Chessie loved math. She secretly wished to be selected for the Math Student of the Month award.

Chessie could piece together a jigsaw puzzle faster than her mom or dad.

Chessie could name the twelve Disciples and all the books of the Bible.

One day, early in the school year, Mrs. Humphrey sadly announced,

"I'm sorry to say that today is my last day. I've been transferred to The Preparatory Institute because they need a geometry specialist, and I'm one of the few in this region ... I will miss you all!"

Tears of disappointment
filled Chessie's eyes.

The Preparatory Institute
was a school Chessie wasn't
allowed to attend.

The next day, Chessie said to her friend Patsy, "It's so unfair. We walk past four other schools before reaching our school, and I bet all those schools have a math teacher."

Once at school, Headmaster Coleman announced, "Children, you deserve the best. While I locate a new math teacher, you will be supervised by Miss Caramel. She is currently a college student who is home for two weeks."

Chessie slowly raised her hand. "Will we still have Student of the Month?"

"I'm sorry, no," Headmaster Coleman responded. "That's on hold until we find a permanent teacher."

Chessie's heart sank. Then she remembered Mrs. Humphrey saying, "You sparkle, Chessie. Keep working hard to help everyone sparkle." Chessie came up with a plan.

On her way home that afternoon, Chessie watched the children playing at The Prep Institute.

"Do you need assistance?" the principal asked.

"I need a math teacher," Chessie responded. "Can you help me?"

"I'm sorry. No," the principal said. "I cannot help you."

LIBRARY

Tutoring
Classes
available
Sign Up
Today.

At the library, Chessie, still determined, spied a tutoring advertisement. Perhaps the librarian could help her! That night, Chessie pulled a blank sheet of paper from her math workbook and composed a letter.

As Chessie trudged home, she remembered her mom and dad saying something about a "league" that helped a family in New York.

"It must be the National Urban League," Chessie thought. "If they helped that family, maybe they can help me and my friends."

Chessie thought long and hard about how to approach the National Urban League. She'd been told "no" twice already, but perhaps that was because she was just one person. Surely the National Urban League couldn't say "no" to a parade of people.

On Saturday, Chessie gathered her friends in front of their school building. Other inquisitive children from the town asked if they could join the march to the National Urban League office.

The children were ready.

With her friends close behind, Chessie strode
into the office.

"Well, well, who do we have here?" the woman at the desk asked.
"We need a math teacher at our school. Can you help us?"

The woman smiled at Chessie.

"What's your name?" she asked.

"Chessie Dentley."

"Well, Chessie, I'm Mrs. Saunders. Math is my favorite subject, too. Wait right here."

Minutes later, Chessie and her friends were led into a large room. The Urban League members looked up from their paperwork.

"That's a big ask," Mr. Ashbee said. He walked to his desk. Chessie followed.

"There is room for two students at another school," Mr Ashbee said.

"Do you want that?" Chessie sighed, "No. I want to help everyone in my school. What about Mrs. Saunders?"

"Well ... Mrs. Saunders works at this office," Mr. Ashbee said. "We'll need to start a local Urban League Chapter. As for getting a math teacher, I'll see what I can do."

Chessie looked up. She had a huge grin on her face. "Really?"

"Really," said Mr. Ashbee.

Two weeks later Chessie sat in a classroom filled with extra books. At the front of the room, Mrs. Saunders drew a polygon on the board.

"Who knows how to determine the area of this five-sided polygon?" Mrs. Saunders asked.

Chessie smiled as numerous hands shot into the air.

The End